For SCBWI, the Ezra Jack Keats Foundation, the de Grummond Children's Literature Collection,
and everyone who was kind to this New Kid —A.D.

For those who dare to be different —E.K.

Published by Roaring Brook Press · Roaring Brook Press is
a division of Holtzbrinck Publishing Holdings Limited Partnership · 120 Broadway,
New York, NY 10271 · mackids.com · Text copyright © 2021 by Ame Dyckman · Illustrations
copyright © 2021 by Eda Kaban · All rights reserved.

Library of Congress Cataloging-in-Publication Data
Names: Dyckman, Ame, author. | Kaban, Eda, illustrator.
Title: The new kid has fleas / written by Ame Dyckman ; illustrated by Eda Kaban.
Description: First edition. | New York: Roaring Brook Press, 2021. | Audience: Ages 3–6. | Audience: Grades K–1. | Summary: When a wild new
student, rumored to have fleas, is paired with the narrator for a science project, she proves there is a lot more to her—and her unusual family—
than anyone could have guessed.
Identifiers: LCCN 2020039931 | ISBN 9781250245243 (hardcover)
Subjects: CYAC: Individuality—Fiction. | Science projects—Fiction. | Schools—Fiction. | Humorous stories.
Classification: LCC PZ7.D9715 New 2021 | DDC [E]—dc23
LC record available at https://lccn.loc.gov/2020039931

Our books may be purchased in bulk for promotional, educational, or business use. Please contact your local bookseller or the Macmillan
Corporate and Premium Sales Department at (800) 221-7945 ext. 5442 or by email at MacmillanSpecialMarkets@macmillan.com.

First edition, 2021 · Book design by Aram Kim · The art for this book was painted digitally. · Printed in China by Hung Hing Off-set Printing Co. Ltd., Heshan City,
Guangdong Province · 10 9 8 7 6 5 4 3 2 1 · No squirrels were harmed in the making of this book.

THE NEW KID HAS FLEAS

Written by **Ame Dyckman**

Illustrated by **Eda Kaban**

Roaring Brook Press
New York

I'm not sure about the New Kid.

Mom and Dad say don't stare.
That I should put myself in her shoes.
But the New Kid doesn't *wear* shoes.
And it's hard not to stare . . .

Especially during Gym.

And Music.

AROOO!

And Lunch.

Molly tells everyone that the New Kid has fleas.
I don't know if she does or not.
I don't ask.

Nobody really talks to the New Kid. But she doesn't care.

Well, I don't think she does.

I wonder who'll choose the New Kid
to be their Science project buddy.
I already chose Stewart.
And Stewart already chose me.

But our teacher says today the bowl will choose.
(We hate it when the bowl chooses.)
Stewart gets paired with . . .

Molly.
Stewart looks like *he*
just ate a squirrel, too.

I'll be okay. As long as I don't get paired with—

We have to work on our project after school.

At *her* house.

I wonder what Stewart will say at my funeral.

The New Kid's parents are home.
Her brother and sisters, too.

Her *little* brother and sisters.

I'm not so nervous about the New Kid's house anymore.

Until . . .

Snack.

It's not bad!

Things are different here.

Bathroom?

I just go with the flow.

We start on our project.
Turns out, the New Kid knows a LOT.

And she's funny. Funnier than Molly or any of us knew.

We make a good team.

And I didn't see a single flea.

I decide to tell Molly
first thing in the morning.

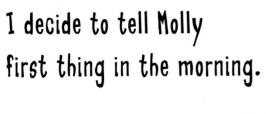

But Molly's not at school.
Stewart says she's home
with lice.

The New Kid and I can't wait to share our project.
Everyone loves it.

Especially us.

It's time to choose an Art project buddy.
Stewart chooses me.

Then our teacher says . . .

We can work in groups of *three*.
Now I'm sure about the New K—

I mean, now I'm sure about Kiki.